The Grains Group

BY BETH BENCE REINKE, MS, RD

The Child's World

Published by The Child's World®
1980 Lookout Drive • Mankato, MN 56003-1705
800-599-READ • www.childsworld.com

Acknowledgments
The Child's World®: Mary Berendes, Publishing Director
Red Line Editorial: Editorial direction
The Design Lab: Design
Amnet: Production
Photographs ©: Front cover: FoodIcons; FoodIcons, 3, 4, 9, 23;
Kalavati/Shutterstock Images, 3, 18, 21; choosemyplate.gov, 5;
GRei/Shutterstock Images, 7; M. Unal Ozmen/Shutterstock Images, 8;
Monkey Business Images/Shutterstock Images, 11; BrandX Images, 12;
Jill Chen/Shutterstock Images, 13; marla dawn studio/Shutterstock
Images, 15; Jiri Hera/Shutterstock Images, 16; subman/iStockphoto, 17;
PhotoDisc, 19

ISBN: 978-1623236045
LCCN: 2013931363

Printed in the United States of America
Mankato, MN
July, 2013
PA02178

ABOUT THE AUTHOR

Beth Bence Reinke is a registered dietitian with a master's degree in nutrition from Penn State University. She uses her background in education and pediatric nutrition to help kids learn about healthy eating. Beth is a member of the Academy of Nutrition and Dietetics, a children's author, a magazine writer, and a columnist for her favorite sport, NASCAR.

Table of Contents

CHAPTER ONE

The Great Grains Group

Amy watched the tiny, gold **kernels**. The kernels jiggled and jumped. *Pop, pop, pop!* They sprouted into white puffs. *Mmm,* the popcorn smelled delicious. *Crunch, crunch!* Amy munched on the popcorn for a snack.

Popcorn goes in the grains section of the MyPlate food guide. The MyPlate guide has a plate and cup that shows how much to eat for meals and snacks. MyPlate helps kids choose healthy foods from all five food groups: dairy, protein, grains, fruits, and vegetables. Grains fill one-fourth of the plate.

▲ **Popcorn is a grain food.**

▶ **Opposite page: The MyPlate guidelines recommend you fill a quarter of your plate with grain foods.**

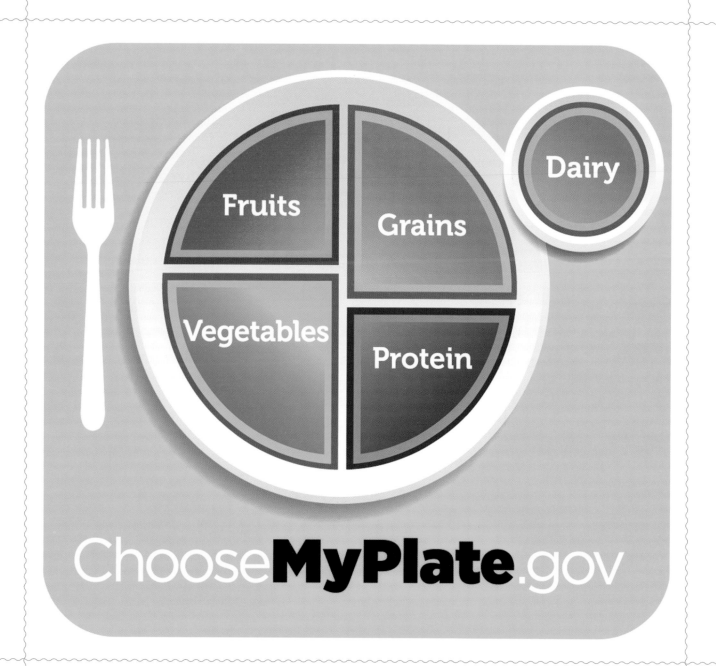

ChooseMyPlate.gov

Many kinds of foods are in the grains group. Bread, pasta, and cereal are grain foods. So are tortillas, crackers, and pancakes. Eating a variety of grain foods helps kids stay healthy. Foods in the grains group come from plants such as corn, wheat, rice, and oats. Grains can be whole or refined.

Whole-grain foods are made from the entire grain kernel. Because **whole grains** have the whole kernel, all of the nutrients are there. That is why whole-grain foods are more nutritious. A grain kernel has three parts: the **bran**, the **germ**, and the **endosperm**. The **fiber** in whole grains comes from the bran. Fiber aids digestion and helps your tummy feel full longer. Fiber also helps protect against some diseases. Whole grains have **vitamins** and **minerals** that help you stay healthy. These nutrients come mostly from the tiny germ and the bran. The largest part of the grain kernel is called

THE GRAIN KERNEL
A grain kernel has three parts: bran, germ, and endosperm. Whole grains contain all three parts of the kernel. The bran is the outer layer. It is full of fiber and B vitamins. The germ is the tiny part inside the kernel. It has lots of B vitamins, vitamin E, minerals, and healthy fats. The bran and germ are small but contain the kernel's nutrients. Whole grains are healthier because they include the bran and germ.

▶ Opposite page: Whole grains are more nutritious because they contain all three parts of a grain kernel.

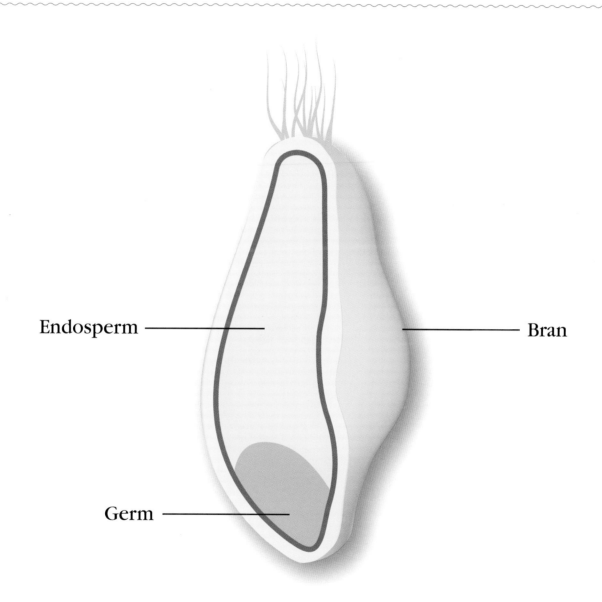

Endosperm ——————————————————
Bran

Germ ——————————

the endosperm. It contains mostly **carbohydrates** that give you energy.

Refined grains have been milled. That means the kernels are crushed and sifted. Then the most nutritious parts are removed—the bran and germ. What is left after milling is the endosperm. Refined grains are made from only the endosperm. Food

◀ **White flour is a refined grain. It is made from the endosperm of a wheat kernel.**

companies like to use refined grains because they make softer foods that last longer.

Many of the grain foods on store shelves contain **enriched grains**. That means iron and a few of the vitamins are added back, but not the fiber. Refined grains are often enriched. That is one reason why MyPlate says to make half of your grains whole. Eating a variety of whole-grain foods provides lots of nutrients to help you stay healthy.

Grains and Labels

Whole grains have more fiber, vitamins, and minerals than refined grains have. That is why MyPlate says to make half of your grains whole grains. But how can you tell which foods are whole grains? Some

▼ It can be hard to tell if a grain food is a whole grain or refined grain.

foods are always whole grains, such as popcorn, oatmeal, wild rice, and brown rice. But a darker color does not always mean a food is a whole grain. Breads or crackers that look brown may be whole grain. But they might be refined grains with molasses or coloring added.

Kids ages four to eight need to eat 4 or 5 ounces of grains each day. Kids ages nine to 13 need 5 or 6 ounces of grains each day. Remember to choose whole grains as often as you can. The following count as 1 ounce of food from the grains group:

- One slice of bread
- 1 cup ready-to-eat cereal
- 1/2 cup cooked rice, cooked pasta, or oatmeal

IS IT A WHOLE GRAIN?
You can tell if a food is made from whole grains. Look on the food's packaging for the ingredients list. The first ingredient is the most important one to check. Do you see the word *whole* before the first ingredient? If the answer is yes, it is a whole-grain food.

▶ **Opposite page: Top your morning oatmeal with some peaches or blueberries.**

CHAPTER TWO

Corn and Wheat

▶ Opposite page: Wrap your favorite meat and vegetables in a corn tortilla for a yummy meal.

Corn and wheat are used in many food products. The top part of a corn or wheat plant that contains the kernels is called the ear. Did you know an ear of corn has about 800 kernels? That is a lot of corn to chew! Corn is unusual because it is both a grain and a fresh vegetable. Corn has lots of vitamin A and other nutrients that are good for your eyes. The following corn foods count as 1 ounce of grains:

- One small corn muffin
- One small corn tortilla
- 3 cups popped popcorn
- 1/2 cup grits

▲ Corn is a whole-grain food and a vegetable.

Wheat is the most common grain used to make breads and pasta in the United States. When you see a bag of all-purpose flour, it is refined wheat flour. MyPlate reminds us to eat more whole grains instead of refined grains. To find whole-grain flour, look for the words *whole wheat* on the bag. For wheat foods, each of the following counts as 1 ounce of grains:

- One slice of bread
- 1/2 cup cooked pasta
- Five whole-wheat crackers
- One pancake 4 to 5 inches (10 to 12 cm) across

Do you help adults shop or cook? Maybe you could suggest ways to eat more whole grains. There are many ways to add corn and whole-wheat foods. Add corn to soups or salads. Make lasagna with whole-grain noodles. Use whole-grain pasta in macaroni and cheese. Snack on popcorn and whole-wheat crackers. Make french toast with whole-wheat bread.

DESSERTS
Many cookies, cakes, and other desserts are made from refined wheat flour. They also contain lots of added sugars and fats. MyPlate reminds us to eat less refined grains, added sugar, and fat. These foods give us energy but few nutrients. Instead, you can eat healthier desserts that taste terrific. Enjoy sweet, juicy fruit. Munch on a whole-grain cereal bar. For a special treat, make everyone's favorite whole-grain cookies—oatmeal!

▶ Opposite page: Whole-grain foods such as these oatmeal cookies can be sweet, too!

CHAPTER THREE

Rice and Oats

Rice and oats are grains, too. They can be eaten as a single food, such as plain rice or oatmeal. Or rice or oats can be ingredients in other foods, such as chicken and rice soup or granola bars. You may have seen white or brown rice. Did you know rice comes in other colors, including red, purple, and black? Grains of rice can be long, medium, or short, too. Wild rice, brown rice, and colored rice are whole grains. But white rice is a refined grain.

Oats are a whole grain. They have a special kind of fiber that helps keep your heart healthy. Oatmeal makes a yummy, hearty breakfast. You can add berries or nuts for extra

▶ **Opposite page: Eat oat cereal in the morning to jump-start your day.**

▲ **Rice is whole-grain food used in many different dishes.**

flavor. Here are some rice and oats foods. Each of these servings counts as 1 ounce of grains:

- 1/2 cup cooked rice
- 1/2 cup cooked oatmeal
- One packet instant oatmeal
- 1 1/4 cups puffed rice cereal
- 1 cup ready-to-eat oat cereal

MyPlate reminds us to make half of our grains whole. You can help your family eat more whole-grain rice and oats.

- Use oatmeal instead of bread crumbs in meatloaf or meatballs.
- Make rice pudding with brown rice.
- Create your own trail mix with ready-to-eat oat cereal, nuts, and dried fruit.
- Buy wild rice or colored rice instead of white rice.
- Make oatmeal cookies or oatmeal muffins.

OTHER GRAINS TO TRY

Corn, wheat, rice, and oats are not the only grains. Have you eaten a tiny, round, white grain called barley? It is cooked and eaten plain or in vegetable soup. You can find barley in boxes at the grocery store. Maybe you have tasted rye bread or buckwheat pancakes. Rye and buckwheat are grains, too. These whole grains also have fiber, vitamins, and minerals. Plus, they taste great!

▶ Opposite page: Rice comes in many varieties.

▲ Granola is a healthy whole-grain snack.

Hands-on Activity: Whole-Grain Trail Mix

Whole grains make great snacks, such as this crunchy trail mix.

What You'll Need:

Measuring cups, a large bowl, a big spoon, four plastic zipper bags, 1 cup oat circle cereal, 1 cup whole-grain oat squares cereal, 1 cup small whole-wheat pretzels, 1/2 cup nuts (peanuts, almonds, or walnuts), 1/2 cup dried fruit (raisins or dried cranberries)

Directions:

1. First, measure your ingredients and dump them all into a large bowl. Stir well.
2. Then divide trail mix evenly into four plastic zipper bags.
3. Serve your homemade, whole-grain snack with a glass of milk. Yum!

Glossary

bran (bran): Bran is the outer layer of a grain kernel. The bran contains fiber and B vitamins.

carbohydrates (kar-bo-HY-drayts): Carbohydrates are parts of food that provide energy to the body. Fiber, starches, and sugars are all carbohydrates.

endosperm (EN-doh-sperm): The endosperm is the largest part of the grain kernel. The endosperm contains mostly carbohydrates for energy.

enriched grains (en-RICH-ed graynz): Enriched grains are refined grains that have iron and a few of the vitamins added back. Many refined grains on store shelves are enriched grains.

fiber (FYE-ber): Fiber is the part of plant foods the body cannot break down. Fiber helps with healthy digestion.

germ (jurm): The germ is the inner layer of a grain kernel. The germ contains B vitamins, vitamin E, minerals, and healthy fats.

kernels (KUR-nilz): Kernels are seeds of corn, wheat, or other grain plant. Kernels contain the bran, endosperm, and germ.

minerals (MIN-er-ulz): Minerals are substances found in foods. Minerals help the body stay healthy.

refined grains (ree-FYEND graynz): Refined grains are foods made with only the part of the grain seed that contains starch. White bread and white pasta are refined grains.

vitamins (VYE-tuh-minz): Vitamins are substances found in foods that help the body stay healthy. Vitamins are found in fruits and vegetables.

whole grains (hol GRAYNZ): Whole grains are foods made with all three parts of the grain seed. Fiber, minerals, and vitamins are found in whole grains.

To Learn More

BOOKS

Levenson, George. *Bread Comes to Life: A Garden of Wheat and a Loaf to Eat*. Berkeley: Tricycle Press, 2004.

Micucci, Charles. *The Life and Times of Corn*. Boston: Houghton Mifflin Books for Children, 2009.

WEB SITES

Visit our Web site for links about the grains food group: childsworld.com/links

Note to Parents, Teachers, and Librarians: We routinely verify our Web links to make sure they are safe and active sites. So encourage your readers to check them out!

Index